A Note to Parents and Caregivers:

Read-it! Readers are for children who are just starting on the amazing road to reading. These beautiful books support both the acquisition of reading skills and the love of books.

The PURPLE LEVEL presents basic topics and objects using high frequency words and simple language patterns.

The RED LEVEL presents familiar topics using common words and repeating sentence patterns.

The BLUE LEVEL presents new ideas using a larger vocabulary and varied sentence structure.

The YELLOW LEVEL presents more challenging ideas, a broad vocabulary, and wide variety in sentence structure.

The GREEN LEVEL presents more complex ideas, an extended vocabulary range, and expanded language structures.

The ORANGE LEVEL presents a wide range of ideas and concepts using challenging vocabulary and complex language structures.

When sharing a book with your child, read in short stretches, pausing often to talk about the pictures. Have your child turn the pages and point to the pictures and familiar words. And be sure to reread favorite stories or parts of stories.

There is no right or wrong way to share books with children. Find time to read with your child, and pass on the legacy of literacy.

Adria F. Klein, Ph.D.
Professor Emeritus
California State University
San Bernardino, California

Editor: Jacqueline A. Wolf
Designer: Nathan Gassman
Page Production: Angela Kilmer
Creative Director: Keith Griffin
Editorial Director: Carol Jones
The illustrations in this book were digitally collaged.

Picture Window Books
5115 Excelsior Boulevard
Suite 232
Minneapolis, MN 55416
877-845-8392
www.picturewindowbooks.com

Printed in the United States of America.

Library of Congress Cataloging-in-Publication Data
Jones, Christianne C.
Willy the worm / by Christianne C. Jones ; illustrated by Zachary Trover.
p. cm. — (Read-it! readers)
ISBN 1-4048-1593-7 (hard cover)
[1. Willie, a silly worm who pays friends to dig holes for him because he hates dirt and
mud, changes his thinking after an accident. 2. Worms—Fiction.] I. Trover, Zachary,
ill. II. Title. III. Series.

PZ7.J6823Wil 2005
[E]—dc22   2005023149

Willy *the* Worm

by Christianne C. Jones
illustrated by Zachary Trover

Special thanks to our advisers for their expertise:

Adria F. Klein, Ph.D.
Professor Emeritus, California State University
San Bernardino, California

Susan Kesselring, M.A.
Literacy Educator
Rosemount–Apple Valley–Eagan (Minnesota) School District

PiCTURE WiNDOW BOOKS
Minneapolis, Minnesota

Worms like dirt. Not Willy.

"Dirt, dirt, dirt. I hate dirt!" Willy said.

His friends didn't understand.

What was wrong with him?

Other worms took mud baths.

Not Willy. He took a clean shower.

Other worms dug their own tunnels.

Not Willy. He paid friends to dig for him.

Other worms crawled through tunnels.

Not Willy. He drove his shiny red car.

Other worms dressed up in dirt.

HOME
SWEET
DIRT

Not Willy. He dressed up in clothes.

On Willy's way home from school one day, it started raining.

"Oh, no! I'm going to ruin my new scarf!" Willy yelled.

The other worms played in the
fresh mud.

Not Willy. He tried to wiggle away.

Willy could see his car.

He was almost to safety.

Suddenly, Willy slipped.

He fell right into a pile of mud.

24

Willy started screaming and crying.
The other worms wiggled over to
help him.

When they saw Willy, they started
to laugh.

Willy was covered in mud.

Willy started to laugh, too.

He actually liked how the mud felt. It was cold and soft.

"Maybe dirt isn't so bad," Willy said.

30

"We told you," said his friends as they jumped into the mud.

More *Read-it!* Readers

Bright pictures and fun stories help you practice your reading skills. Look for more books at your level.

Back to School 1-4048-1166-4
The Bath 1-4048-1576-7
The Best Snowman 1-4048-0048-4
Bill's Baggy Pants 1-4048-0050-6
Camping Trip 1-4048-1167-2
Days of the Week 1-4048-1581-3
Eric Won't Do It 1-4048-1188-5
Fable's Whistle 1-4048-1169-9
Finny Learns to Swim 1-4048-1582-1
Goldie's New Home 1-4048-1171-0
I Am in Charge of Me 1-4048-0646-6
The Lazy Scarecrow 1-4048-0062-X
Little Joe's Big Race 1-4048-0063-8
The Little Star 1-4048-0065-4
Meg Takes a Walk 1-4048-1005-6
The Naughty Puppy 1-4048-0067-0
Paula's Letter 1-4048-1183-4
Selfish Sophie 1-4048-0069-7
The Tall, Tall Slide 1-4048-1186-9
The Traveling Shoes 1-4048-1588-0
A Trip to the Zoo 1-4048-1590-2

Looking for a specific title or level? A complete list of *Read-it!* Readers is available on our Web site:

www.picturewindowbooks.com